Can David Do It?

Can David Do It?

by Sandy Asher

Illustrated
by Mark Alan Weatherby

A
LITTLE APPLE
PAPERBACK

SCHOLASTIC INC.

New York Toronto London Auckland Sydney

ISBN 0-590-43837-9

Copyright © 1991 by Sandy Asher.
Illustrations copyright © 1991 by Scholastic Inc.
All rights reserved. Published by Scholastic Inc.
APPLE PAPERBACKS is a registered trademark of Scholastic Inc.

12 11 10 9 8 7 6 5 4 3 2 1   1 2 3 4 5 6/9

Printed in the U.S.A.   40

First Scholastic printing, March 1991

For the pioneering staff of
Allens Lane Art Center Day Camp

Contents

Can David Do It?

Chapter One
Soldiers and Mice

"I'll get it!" David shouted. He caught the phone on the second ring.

"David? It's Ellie," said the voice at the other end.

"Hi, Ellie! What's up?"

Ellie Bell was David's best friend. She lived right next door. David and Ellie went to Rountree School together. They were both in Mr. Crane's third-grade class.

"Can you come over?" Ellie asked. "Mary and Pat are here. We're playing Nutcracker ballet."

Mary Stone and Pat Parker were in Mr.

Crane's class, too. On Saturdays, they went to Ballet One with Ellie. David watched their class once, on Visiting Day. It was fun.

Monday night, Ellie, Mary, and Pat tried out for the *Nutcracker* ballet. It was all they could talk about lately — being in a real ballet on a real stage.

"I'll be right over," David said.

He hung up the phone. Then he peeked into his father's study. Mr. Sims sat at his desk, grading papers. He taught science at Central High School.

David's mom didn't get home until after five o'clock. She worked for a computer company. David checked the clock on his father's desk. It was only 4:15 now.

"I'm going to Ellie's for a while," he said.

Mr. Sims looked up from his pile of papers. "Do you have homework?" he asked.

"Just a little math," David said.

Mr. Sims gave him a funny look. One

eyebrow rose high over his silver glasses. "Just a little math?" he asked.

David wasn't very good at math. When Mr. Crane's third-grade class did regular math in their regular room, David went to special math. Ralph Major sometimes called it "dummy math." Ralph was David's other best friend. But not when he said things like that.

"I'll do it right after supper," David promised.

"All right," Mr. Sims said. "Be home by six."

"Okay!" David raced out the back door and over to Ellie's. He had almost two hours to play.

Ellie, Pat, and Mary were waiting for him. They had Ellie's living room furniture pushed back to the walls.

"Come on, David!" Ellie said. "We're practicing for the *Nutcracker*."

"You just tried out last night," David said. "Do you know your dances already?"

"No," Ellie said. "Just what parts we play. We don't start rehearsals until next week. Mary doesn't even know what part she has yet. She has to go to another audition tonight."

"Let's not talk about that," Mary said. "It makes me too nervous."

"You *will* get a part, won't you?" David asked her.

"I don't know," Mary said, very softly. "Nobody said anything about that last night. They just said I have to come back tonight."

"Of course you'll get a part," Ellie said. "You're the best dancer in Ballet One."

"Ellie and I got *two* parts," Pat reminded David. "We're going to be mice and gingerbread cookies."

"Mary will probably get *three* parts," Ellie said.

"I don't think so," Mary said.

"Well, for right now, you can pretend to be a soldier," Ellie told her. "You, too, David. Last night, we learned a little bit of the battle between the mice and the wooden soldiers. Pat and I are the mice. Okay?"

"Sure," David said. "What do I do?"

"You march," Mary told him. She marched around the room on stiff legs. Tall and thin, she looked just like a wooden soldier.

David tried to do the same thing.

"You're good at it, David!" Mary said.

"Ellie shows me Ballet One stuff all the time," David said. "It's just like follow-the-leader."

"And then the mice attack!" Ellie cried.

She and Pat skittered across the room. They held their hands up like paws and jabbed at the soldiers.

"When the mice attack, the soldiers march away," Pat said. Her two bunches of yellow curls bounced around as she talked.

David and Mary marched backward into a corner.

"Then the soldiers draw their swords," Mary said. She pretended to pull out a sword. So did David. "When the soldiers attack, the mice run away."

David and Mary chased Ellie and Pat. Soon the mice were trapped between the sofa and the wall.

Back and forth they went. First the mice were winning. Then the soldiers were winning. Then the mice were winning again.

"But the soldiers win in the end," Mary said. "That's how the story goes. And the mice fall down dead!"

Mary swung her pretend sword high in the air. Then she swooped it down at Ellie. Ellie flopped onto the floor.

"Ahhhhh!" she yelled. "I'm dead!" Her glasses slipped down her nose. A barrette popped out of her dark hair. But she lay perfectly still, with her eyes closed.

"My turn to win!" David said.

He swung his pretend sword and chased Pat around the room. He was having so much fun, it was hard not to smile. But a wooden soldier couldn't do that. So he scowled at Pat.

"Wait!" she cried. "Not all the mice die. Some of them have to drag the dead ones off the stage."

"Oh," David said. "Okay." He stood at attention.

Pat grabbed Ellie's feet and dragged her across the carpet. At the dining room door, she said, "The end!"

Ellie's eyes popped open and she sat up.

"That was fun!" David said. "Let's do it again!"

Mary shook her head. "I can't. My mom will be here soon. I have to go to that audition after dinner. I wish you could all come with me."

"We already have our parts," Pat reminded her.

"David doesn't," Ellie said. "He could try out."

David looked at the three faces watching him. They were hoping he'd say yes. But he shook his head no.

"I have math homework," he explained. Dumb old dummy math!

Chapter Two
The Math Whiz
and the Science Whiz

Mrs. Sims heaped salad onto David's plate. "You and I have to go shopping after dinner," she said. "You need a new jacket."

"What for?" David asked.

"Tomorrow is Franny's big night," Mrs. Sims explained. "The Honors Assembly at her school. You've outgrown your best jacket. Your wrists hang right out of the sleeves."

"Ah, Mama, it's okay," David said. "I can just pull my arms up a little. Nobody will look at me anyway. They'll all be looking at Franny."

Franny was David's big sister. She was a senior at Parkview High School, and she was smart. That was why they were going to the Honors Assembly. Franny was getting an award for being so smart.

David's brother, J.T., was smart, too. People always said, "Franny is a science whiz, and J.T. is a math whiz." J.T. was away at college. David missed him a lot.

"David has math homework to do," Mr. Sims said.

"It won't take us long to shop," Mrs. Sims told him. "There's a sale at Kids 'n' Style. We'll be back in plenty of time for math."

David groaned. "Math *and* shopping," he muttered. He stabbed his fork into a cherry tomato. Juice squirted across his plate.

"What I can't figure out," said Mrs. Sims, "is why math is so hard for you, David. Franny and J.T. enjoy it."

David shrugged. "I guess I'd enjoy it, too," he said, "if I could do it."

His parents laughed. "You keep working at it, son," Mr. Sims said. "You'll catch on."

David didn't think so. He thought maybe Ralph was right. Maybe he *was* a "dummy math" dummy. He pushed his salad around his plate until dinner was over.

Then he followed his mother out to the car. It was already dark outside. Campbell Street was bright with lights all the way to the South Oaks Shopping Center.

Three stores away from Kids 'n' Style was Miss Drew's School of Dance. "That's where Ellie goes to Ballet One," David said.

Mrs. Sims pulled into a parking spot. "It seems to be closed tonight," she said.

"Miss Drew is probably at the audition for the *Nutcracker* ballet," David said. "I know Mary Stone is."

Mrs. Sims hurried David out of the car and into Kids 'n' Style. He didn't tell her that Mary had wanted him to go to the audition. He tried not to think about the fun Mary was having. But he couldn't help wondering if people who were dumb at math would be dumb at ballet, too.

"Stop daydreaming," Mrs. Sims said. She handed David a blue jacket. "Try this one on."

David took off his coat and put the jacket on. He looked at himself in the mirror while his mother tugged at the sleeves.

He didn't *look* dumb. In fact, he looked a lot like J.T. They were both tall and dark chocolate-brown, with dimples and bright black eyes. "A fine-looking bunch of children," Grandpa Sims always said. "Smart, too."

David figured he mostly meant J.T. and Franny.

His mother handed him another jacket. "Try this one," she said. After he put it on, she stepped back and looked it over.

"Mama," David said, "how come Franny's a science whiz and J.T.'s a math whiz and I'm not any kind of whiz at all?"

"Oh, you're some kind of whiz," Mrs. Sims said. "But you're only in third grade."

"Were Franny and J.T. in special math when they were in third grade?" David asked.

"No," Mrs. Sims said. "But science and math are their best subjects. Everybody's best at something."

Everybody but me, David thought.

His mother held up the first jacket again. "Do you like it?" she asked.

"It's okay, I guess."

"Then we'll take it."

Mrs. Sims paid for the jacket and David carried it out to the parking lot. He hopped into the car and watched the Campbell Street lights flash by again as his mother drove home.

"Can you have a dumb brain if everybody

else in your family is smart?" he asked his mother.

"You don't have a dumb brain, David," Mrs. Sims said. "You have a fine brain. Math is hard for a lot of people. Now, just stop worrying about it, okay?"

"Okay."

David knew that was what his mother wanted him to say. But he didn't think he would ever stop worrying about it.

Chapter Three
News from the Nutcracker

David peered through the kitchen door curtain. Ellie was jumping up and down on the porch. He let her in.

"Mary's going to be Clara!" she squealed. "She got home from the audition too late to call last night. But she just called now. Can you believe it?"

"Who's Clara?" David asked.

"The star of the whole *Nutcracker* ballet," Ellie explained. "Well, the child star. Not the grown-up star. But a *star!*"

"That's great!" David said.

He grabbed his coat and bookbag and told his mother he was leaving. Then he and Ellie headed for school. A cold November wind stung their faces.

"Remember Miss Drew? Our Ballet One teacher?" Ellie went on. "She's going to be the grown-up star. The Sugar Plum Fairy. And guess what? Mr. Crane was picked to play Clara's uncle!"

"*Our* Mr. Crane?" David gasped. "Our *teacher?*"

"Yes!" Ellie said. "Mary danced with him at the audition."

David and Ellie raced through the gate, up the stairs, and into Rountree School. The warmth inside felt good.

"There they are!" Ellie shouted.

Mrs. Long, the principal, looked out of her office door. "Keep your voice down, Ellie," she said.

But Ellie was already flying down the

17

hall toward Mary and Pat. David hurried after her.

"That's great news, Mary," he said, as Ellie caught her in a giant hug.

Pat moved a few steps away.

"Thank you," Mary said, blushing beneath her freckles.

"Is Mr. Crane *really* in the *Nutcracker*?" Ellie asked.

Mary giggled. "Uh-huh."

"I can't imagine Mr. Crane *dancing*," David said.

"We waltzed," Mary told him. "He was good."

Pat never said a word. She just chewed on one of her yellow curls and frowned. David wondered why, but there was no time to ask. The bell rang.

The four of them headed for their room. Mr. Crane was at his desk, grinning from ear to ear. David had never seen him with a smile that big.

Mr. Crane was a good teacher. He was strict, but fair. He never yelled. But he didn't smile much, either.

"Good morning, third-graders!" he said when everyone was seated. He made a song out of it: "Gooooood morrrninggggg!"

"He sounds like a cow mooing," Ralph Major whispered.

Ralph sat beside David, in the first seat in the first row. Ellie sat behind Ralph.

"Something exciting happened to me last night," Mr. Crane went on. "I was given a part in the *Nutcracker* ballet. I've always thought it would be fun to be in a ballet. And now, I am!"

"Ballet?" Ralph yelped. "Yuck!" He stuck a finger into his mouth and pretended to throw up.

Mr. Crane didn't even shoot Ralph a hard look. That was what he usually did when Ralph acted up. First the look. Then Ralph had to move his desk up next to Mr.

Crane's. Then Ralph had to go to Mrs. Long's office.

But this time, Mr. Crane just went on smiling. "That's right, Ralph," he said. "Ballet. You may say 'yuck' all you want. I *like* ballet."

"Yuck-yuck-yuck-yuck-yuck — " Ralph began.

Mr. Crane's face turned just a tiny bit hard. "You may say it all you want to *yourself*, Ralph."

Ralph covered his mouth with both hands. David could still hear tiny "yucks" coming through his fingers. Sometimes Ralph was really funny.

But Mr. Crane was too excited about the *Nutcracker* to notice.

"What part did you get, Mr. Crane?" Kim Reed asked.

Mr. Crane puffed his chest out proudly. He straightened his red-checked bow tie.

"I'm Dr. Drosselmeyer," he said. "I give the nutcracker doll to my niece, Clara. That's the second part of my wonderful news, third-graders. Clara will be played by your classmate, Mary Stone. Stand up, Mary!"

Mary stood up, blushing bright red. The class cheered and clapped their hands. Ralph whistled. It was so loud, David had to cover his ears.

Mr. Crane shot Ralph the hard look. Ralph got quiet, and so did everyone else. Mary sat down.

"There are two more third-graders in the *Nutcracker* ballet," Mr. Crane went on. "Ellie Bell and Pat Parker, will you please stand up?" Ellie and Pat stood up.

"I know what they're going to be," Ralph called out. "I heard them talking about it yesterday. Rats and crumbs."

"Mice and gingerbread cookies, Ralph!" said Mr. Crane.

But it was too late. The whole class burst out laughing at Ellie and Pat.

"Quit it, Ralph!" David hissed. Sometimes Ralph could be a real pest.

"Rats and crumbs!" Jimmy Duke shouted, and the laughter got louder.

Pat sat down hard. Then she burst into tears.

"Oh, Pat, don't cry," Mary said, trying to comfort her.

"Oh, what do *you* care!" Pat snapped. "You're *Clara*. Nobody's laughing at *you*." She buried her face in her arms.

Now Mary looked as if she might cry, too.

Ellie grabbed Ralph's ear and pinched it.

"Ow!" he yelled.

"Third-graders," Mr. Crane said. "I can't believe how rude you are being this morning. I was going to invite the entire class to see the ballet next month. But now, I'm not sure I want to do that. No, I'm not sure at all."

The class got very quiet again. Mr. Crane turned and wrote the math pages on the board. "You may get to work now," he said.

His *Nutcracker* smile was gone.

Chapter Four
Special Math

"Everybody stand up, please," said Mrs. Ortiz.

There were three round tables in the special math room. David, Jimmy Duke, and Kim Reed always sat together at the table near the window. They were the only ones from Mr. Crane's room in special math. They looked at each other and shrugged their shoulders. Then they stood up.

"I'm going to divide you into teams today," Mrs. Ortiz went on. "Each team member will help the others on the team with their work."

"Isn't that cheating?" Jimmy asked.

"Not when you're *supposed* to work together," Mrs. Ortiz explained. She tapped her pencil on the table near her desk. "David, I'd like you to move up here," she said. She scooted away the two fourth-graders already at that table.

David moved over.

Mrs. Ortiz moved everyone in the room around. A second-grader named Eddie and a fourth-grader, Trudy, ended up at David's table with him.

Eddie had big green eyes. He looked scared. Trudy had red hair in a ponytail. They all looked around the room at the other tables. Nobody knew what to do next.

"All right, teams," Mrs. Ortiz said. "Your first job is to check last night's homework. Start with the second-grader on your team and go up the grades. If you have questions, I'm still here to help."

"This is weird," Eddie said.

"It is," Trudy agreed. "But I think I like it. Three heads are better than one."

David didn't know what to think. He'd never been in a class where everybody could help you with your homework. He didn't think he'd be much help to Eddie and Trudy. They'd be better off with Franny or J.T. on their team.

"You're first, Eddie," Trudy said. "Let's see your homework."

Eddie slid his paper and math book toward the center of the table. Trudy and David scooted their chairs closer to his. David grinned as he read the old second-grade math book. The problems were *easy!*

"I don't get it," Eddie said.

David and Trudy helped him.

Then it was David's turn to show his work. "Maybe I should go last," he said.

"We have to go in order," Trudy insisted. "Mrs. Ortiz said so."

"I went first," Eddie reminded him. "Going first is the hardest."

"Oh, okay." David tore his homework page out of his notebook. It was smudged all over.

"Wow! You erase a lot!" Eddie said. "Even more than *me!*"

"But not enough," Trudy added. "I still see mistakes." She pointed at a problem.

"Even I know five plus four equals nine," said Eddie. "Not seven."

"And you forgot to regroup your tens," Trudy pointed out.

David sighed. "I always make dumb mistakes like that."

"Why?" Eddie asked.

"I just do," David answered. "I put down the number I think is right. But it doesn't *look* right. So I erase it and try another one. And that one doesn't look right either."

"We'd better start your homework all over," Trudy decided.

David went back to problem one. Every time he wrote a number, Trudy and Eddie checked it.

"Right," Trudy said.

David was never sure.

"Don't erase," Eddie warned him.

"Next problem," Trudy said.

Finally David was finished. All the answers were right this time. That felt good.

"Guess I'm next," Trudy said.

"I can't help you," Eddie told her. "I can hardly do *second*-grade math."

David pulled Trudy's homework over. "Look!" he said. "It's not so different. Just more columns, that's all."

Eddie looked at Trudy's homework. "I guess five plus four equals nine in fourth grade, too," he said.

"It's still hard," Trudy insisted.

"If you can do mine, you can do yours," David told her.

"*We* can do it!" Eddie piped up.

And they did.

"Time is just about up," Mrs. Ortiz announced.

"That was the world's fastest math class!" Eddie cried.

"Can we work with our teams every day?" Kim Reed asked.

Mrs. Ortiz nodded. "For a while. We'll see how well it goes."

"You know what's funny about David, Mrs. Ortiz?" Trudy said. "He can do Eddie's

work and my work. But he keeps erasing
his own."

Mrs. Ortiz looked at David with wide,
surprised eyes.

Uh-oh, David thought. Now what?

Chapter Five
Everything's Ruined

What was Mrs. Ortiz thinking? David wondered. He was *supposed* to help his team, wasn't he? Or did he get that wrong, too?

There was no time to find out. Special math was over for the day. Mrs. Ortiz lined the class up and led them into the hall. Just then, Mr. Crane's class came by on their way to recess. Ellie grabbed David's arm as the two lines passed each other.

"I have to talk to you," she said.

"Third-graders walk with their eyes open and their mouths closed," Mr. Crane called from the head of his line.

"My group, stay in line, please," Mrs. Ortiz said.

David shrugged at Ellie. He had to follow the special math group to Mr. Crane's classroom door.

"David, Jimmy, and Kim, get your coats and go right outside to recess," Mrs. Ortiz told them. "The rest of you, come with me." The line went on to the other classrooms.

Inside Mr. Crane's room, David grabbed his coat, hat, and gloves. Then he charged down the hall, buttoning up as he ran.

"Walk, please," said Mrs. Long, turning the corner just in time to catch him.

David walked the rest of the way to the door. Fast. Ellie was waiting for him outside, right at the bottom of the stairs.

"Everything's ruined!" she said. "Pat feels bad about being called a rat and a crumb. Mary feels bad about being Clara because Pat is jealous of her. And I'm not sure how

I feel about anything. But it's not *good*."

David glanced across the yard. It was still cold out. But the sun was shining, and the wind had died down. Mary was over by the swings, alone. Her hands were in her coat pockets, and her head was down.

Pat was huddled with a group of girls near the side of the building. The other girls were talking. But Pat was facing away from them. She still looked ready to cry.

Ralph was nowhere in sight.

"We had a fight while we were getting our coats," Ellie went on. "Mary said she was sorry Ralph had called us rats and crumbs. Then Pat said she guessed Mary was really proud of herself now, being Clara. And Mary said being Clara was ruined if it made her friends angry at her."

"What did *you* say?" David asked.

"That we should be happy just *being* in a real ballet," Ellie said. "But Pat said she wasn't happy at all. She wants to quit!"

"Quitting's dumb," David said. "You're not going to quit, are you?"

"I don't know," Ellie said. "Mary said it wouldn't be any fun if Pat quit. Pat said she didn't care. Then Mr. Crane made us be quiet and get in line."

Suddenly Ralph was beside them. "Talking to a rat, David?" he asked.

Ellie pushed Ralph away. "Shut up, Ralph!"

Ralph pushed her back. David grabbed Ralph's arm. But Ralph tripped him and dragged him to the ground.

"Quit it!" Ellie yelled. She jumped on Ralph's back.

Now David had two people on top of him! "Get off, Ellie!" he gasped.

The weight lifted. David saw Ellie's sneakers bouncing around near his face. "Get him, David!" she cried.

Soon there was a crowd of sneakers and shoes dancing in front of him. "Fight!" someone shouted. Everyone cheered.

David pushed and tugged until Ralph toppled over. He threw himself on Ralph's chest and pinned him to the ground.

"Take it back, Ralph," he said. "Ellie's not a rat."

"She is, too," Ralph insisted. "And you're a dummy."

A hand grabbed David's coat by the collar and yanked him up to his feet. "The fight is over, third-graders," Mr. Crane announced.

He made David and Ralph stand on opposite sides of the steps for the rest of recess. When he left, they crossed their eyes and wiggled their tongues at each other.

Ralph had started the fight. First it made David angry. Then it made him laugh. That was how it always was with Ralph. Trouble ended up in jokes, and jokes ended up in trouble.

Chapter Six
Franny's Big Night

"We'll use my mama's lace tablecloth," Mrs. Sims announced that evening. "And our best dishes." She was so busy planning Franny's big night, she forgot to ask how David's day had gone. That was lucky.

By the time David had the table set, Franny was home from school.

"Hot apple cobbler with vanilla ice cream," he told her. "All your favorites tonight!"

Franny laughed and planted a noisy kiss on his cheek. *"All right!"* she said. Then she took the stairs two at a time. "I'm going to

37

change clothes. Where's that new jacket of yours?"

David charged up the stairs after her. In a flash, they were both in and out of their rooms and dressed in their best clothes. Their parents and Grandpa Sims met them down in the living room.

"Two fine-looking children," Grandpa Sims said, hugging them both at once. "Smart, too!"

Soon they were all settled at the table, passing around Franny's favorite food.

"Too bad J.T. couldn't be here," Grandpa Sims said.

"That's true," Mr. Sims agreed. "But he couldn't miss his classes."

"He'll be home in three weeks," Franny reminded them. "We'll have him for four whole days at Thanksgiving."

"That'll be something to be thankful for, won't it?" Grandpa Sims said.

Three weeks until J.T. came home! David couldn't wait. J.T. had been away at college since August.

Just as David was licking the last bit of ice cream off his spoon, the phone rang. "I'll get it!" he cried, and took off for the kitchen.

"Hello?"

"David! How's it going, little brother?"

"J.T.!" David yelped.

"I'm calling to congratulate Franny," J.T. said. "But first, tell me how you're doing."

J.T.'s voice sounded loud and clear. For a moment, David thought maybe he wasn't miles away at college.

"I'm fine," David said. Suddenly he felt shy. His brother *was* far away. He had new friends and even a new room to sleep in.

"How's third grade treating you?" J.T. wanted to know.

"It's okay," David said.

"Just okay?" J.T. asked. "Not great?"

David wanted to tell J.T. about special math. And about how Ellie and Mary and Pat were fussing at each other. And how Ralph could be fun sometimes and mean other times. But J.T. had important college things to think about now.

"It's fine," David said.

"Well, good," said J.T. "Let me talk to Franny now. See you soon."

J.T. talked to Franny and to everyone else, too. Then it was time to drive to Parkview High School for the Honors Assembly. Franny and David sat beside Grandpa Sims in the backseat.

"Are you nervous, Franny?" David asked.

"A little," Franny said.

"There's nothing to be nervous about," Grandpa Sims told her. "All this family has to do tonight is be proud!"

David felt proud, all right. And excited,

too. He liked visiting Franny's school.

Parkview was a lot bigger than Rountree. Long rows of glass windows spilled light across the parking lot as David and his family pulled up. They quickly joined the other families hurrying up the path toward the big glass doors. Now and then, someone called out, "Hi, Franny!" and Franny waved back.

Inside, a stream of people flowed toward the auditorium. Mr. Sims found four seats together. Franny said, "See you later!" and went to sit up on the stage.

A man spoke into the microphone and everyone got quiet.

"That's Franny's principal," Mrs. Sims whispered. "His name is Mr. Evans."

Mr. Evans talked for a long time. Then he began reading a list of names. As each name was called, a student stood up and crossed the stage to shake his hand. Each student got an award, and everyone applauded.

"Here she comes," Grandpa Sims whispered.

David strained his neck to see better. Sure enough, Franny was walking toward Mr. Evans. "First in science, with a straight-A average," he said. "Francine Sims."

David held his breath. Mr. Evans handed Franny her award. Everyone clapped their hands for her. David and his parents and Grandpa Sims grinned and grinned. It felt fine to have a sister up on that stage with all those smart kids.

Then Mr. Evans called another name. And another. There were awards for writing and art and history and more. The list went on and on.

Were all those people as smart as Franny? David wondered. Was *everyone* in high school as smart as Franny? What happened to kids who weren't? Did they stay back in special math forever?

Chapter Seven
Something's Up

"Good work, David," Mrs. Ortiz said.

It was Friday morning, and she was bent over David's table in special math. She stayed a long time, listening and watching. Finally she moved to another table.

"Why does she keep watching us like that?" Trudy asked.

"I don't know," David said. "It makes me nervous."

"She did the same thing yesterday," Trudy remembered.

"Something's up," Eddie said.

David liked working with Eddie and Trudy. They made him feel kind of smart when he helped them. And he didn't erase much at all when they helped him.

Ralph was wrong when he called it "dummy math," David decided. Eddie and Trudy weren't dumb. They were nice.

Ralph was wrong about the rats and crumbs, too. He just couldn't tell funny jokes from hurting jokes. David wished Pat knew that. He tried to tell her, but she wouldn't listen. She was still sulking. And Mary was sad. And Ellie didn't know what to do. Nothing had changed since Wednesday.

Suddenly Mrs. Ortiz knelt beside David's chair. "David," she said, "would you mind missing recess this morning? I need you to stay here with me."

"Okay," David said.

Now he would have to wait until lunch to see how Ellie was doing.

45

"Thank you," Mrs. Ortiz said.

She asked him to stay in his seat while she returned the others to their regular rooms. When she got back, she gave him a new sheet of paper. It had rows and rows of math problems on it.

"I'd like you to try these for me, David," she said.

"Alone?" David asked.

"Yes," said Mrs. Ortiz. "This time, alone."

David looked at the problems. They were just addition and subtraction. He thought he knew how to do them.

He was *almost* sure he knew how. He tried the first problem. But as soon as he wrote the answer down, it looked wrong. He erased it and tried again. That answer looked worse. He erased again.

His heart began to pound. His hands felt sweaty. They stuck to the paper and made ugly smudges. The places he'd erased looked awful, too. The messier the page got, the worse David felt. It was just like being in regular math again. He wished Eddie and Trudy were there.

He subtracted eight from thirteen and wrote "five." He erased it. The eraser tore right through the paper.

Mrs. Ortiz took the paper away. David felt terrible. He thought he knew that stuff! What was the matter with him?

Mrs. Ortiz patted his shoulder. "It's all right, David," she said.

"I think I could do it with my team," David told her.

"I think you could, too," Mrs. Ortiz agreed. "I have a feeling special math isn't what you need. I'd like to talk it over with Mr. Crane and Mrs. Long. And your parents, too. Maybe we could all meet here at school on Monday morning. Would that be all right with you?"

David nodded. He knew that was what Mrs. Ortiz wanted him to do. But it wasn't all right. Why didn't Mrs. Ortiz think he needed special math? Was he so dumb he needed a math class all to himself?

Chapter Eight
Watching Ballet One

"Will you come to Ballet One with me today?" Ellie asked.

It was Saturday. David and Ellie were in David's room, playing cards. But they kept forgetting whose turn it was. They were too busy thinking about Mary, Pat, Ralph, and special math.

"Is it another Visiting Day?" David asked.

"No," said Ellie. "Just a regular day. But I'm afraid Mary and Pat will tell Miss Drew they're quitting the *Nutcracker*. What will I do then?"

"I don't know," David said. People problems were even harder than math problems. He wished everyone would stop asking him questions he didn't know the answers to!

"Just come with me," Ellie said. "Okay? Please?"

"Okay," David said.

For the first time since Wednesday, Ellie's face lit up with a smile. That made David feel good. Maybe he wasn't the smartest person in the world, but he knew how to be a friend.

After lunch, he rode to the South Oaks Shopping Center with Ellie and her dad. David thought about the big cheerful room where Miss Drew taught Ballet One. Then he thought about staying home, worrying about what Mrs. Ortiz would tell his parents Monday morning. Ballet One was much more fun!

Mr. Bell let them off at Miss Drew's

School of Dance. Inside, Miss Drew remembered David from Visiting Day.

"Welcome back, David," she said.

David had forgotten how pretty Miss
Drew was. Her smile made him feel shy.
She led him to a folding chair near the
piano.

"Mr. Ross," she said to the man playing
the piano, "you remember Ellie's friend,
David Sims, don't you?"

Mr. Ross ran his fingers up and down
the piano keys. It made a happy sound, like
dancing raindrops. David thought that was
a neat way to say hello.

Just then, Mary and Pat came in. Ellie
threw David a worried look. Mary and Pat
said "hi," but they still looked like storm
clouds.

Ellie stayed close to David until class
began. Mary sat near the wall of mirrors to
put on her ballet shoes. Pat sat on the other

side of the room, underneath the *barre*.

David knew the *barre* was what dancers held on to for their warm-up exercises. He knew a lot about Ballet One. He even remembered the names of the other students who came in. Miss Drew had introduced them on Visiting Day. And Ellie talked about them at home, when she taught him the steps she learned each week.

Miss Drew called the class to the *barre*. Mary and Pat stood near Ellie. But they didn't even look at each other. Ellie turned around and made a face at David. He shrugged his shoulders and wished he could tell her what to do.

"Where's Lynn?" the boy named Paul asked Miss Drew.

The pretty smile faded from Miss Drew's face. "Lynn won't be coming to Ballet One anymore," she said.

"Why not?" Nancy asked.

"I know why," Rosa said. "She quit.

Because her mom and dad wouldn't let her try out for the *Nutcracker*. She gets sick a lot. Her mom said it would be too hard for her."

"But why did she quit Ballet One?" Ellie asked.

"Lynn *loves* Ballet One," Mary said.

"We don't even do the *Nutcracker* here," Stanley pointed out. "We go to rehearsals for that."

"She's going to miss all the fun," Ellie said. "Classes and Visiting Days — "

"And our recital in the spring," Pat added.

"And *us*," Mary said. "Her friends."

"She forgot all the good things because of one bad thing!" David cried.

Mary, Ellie, and Pat looked at each other. Then they looked at the floor. David slapped his hand over his mouth. He didn't want Miss Drew to ask him to leave.

But she agreed with him. "That's exactly

right, David," she said. "It's hard when your friends are excited about something and you feel left out. But Lynn gave up all the good things because of one bad thing. That's really very sad, isn't it?"

Ellie looked up from the floor. She stole a glance at David. Then she held out her hands to Mary and Pat.

"Friends?" she asked.

"Friends," Mary said, and held her hands out, too.

Pat scrunched up her mouth for a minute, thinking it over. Then she linked hands with the others.

"Friends," she agreed.

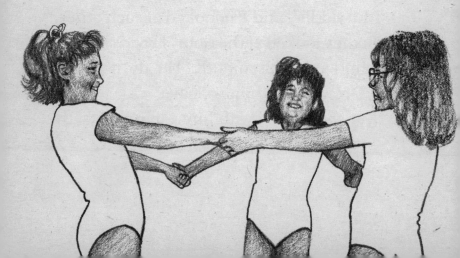

"What's happening here?" Miss Drew asked.

Ellie, Mary, and Pat giggled and dropped hands. They hopped back into line at the *barre*.

David sighed happily as the class began. A lot of good things happen at Ballet One, he thought. Dancing. Music. Miss Drew. Mr. Ross. Visiting Days. Recitals. The *Nutcracker*. Friends.

He watched the class do all the steps Ellie had shown him: *pliés, tendues, petits battements*. Front, side, back, side, they brushed their feet across the floor. David could hardly keep his own feet still.

"Would you like to join us, David?" Miss Drew asked.

"No, thank you," David whispered shyly.

But he wished he could.

Chapter Nine
The Monday Morning Meeting

"Good morning," said Mrs. Long. She shook hands with David's parents. Then she led them all into her office. "Please sit down."

The office was crowded. Mr. Crane and Mrs. Ortiz sat on one side. David and his parents sat on the other. Mrs. Long leaned against her desk.

David felt very small among all the grownups. The oatmeal he had eaten for breakfast made his stomach ache. He bit his lip and peered around the room. Everyone looked very serious.

Mrs. Long turned toward his parents.

"As you know," she said, "David's been in special math for several weeks."

"Math has always been hard for David," Mrs. Sims said. "But he works at it. He really tries."

"He certainly does," Mr. Crane agreed.

"Sometimes he tries so hard," Mrs. Ortiz added, "he erases through his paper."

The grown-ups laughed. It wasn't *mean* laughing. Not the way Ralph laughed. But it still made David squirm in his seat.

Mrs. Ortiz went on talking. "When David helps his team, he has no trouble at all. His own work goes smoothly with the group, too. But when he's asked to work alone, it's back to the eraser again."

"Why do you think that happens, David?" Mr. Sims asked.

The grown-ups stared at David, waiting for his answer. His face burned. He lowered his eyes and watched his sneakers swing back and forth under his chair.

"Is it Ralph?" Mrs. Long asked. "I know he teases you. Is that what upsets you?"

"No," David said, "it's not Ralph."

"Then what is it?" his father asked.

"I just want to be like J.T. and Franny," David whispered. "I just want to get all the answers *right*."

"I don't understand," Mrs. Long said.

David felt his mother take a deep breath beside him. "I think I do," she said. She put her arm around David and pulled him close. "David's brother and sister are excellent math students," she told the others. "He worries about not being as smart as they are."

"David *can* do the work," Mrs. Ortiz said. "But he erases *correct* answers!"

"I'm never *sure*," David tried to explain.

"Maybe it's not *being* smart enough that matters," Mr. Sims said. "Maybe it's *feeling* smart enough."

59

The other grown-ups nodded in agreement.

"Franny and J.T. will always be ahead of you in school, David," Mrs. Sims said. "They can't help it. They're older."

"I know," David said.

"And you'll always be behind them, won't you?" his father asked softly. "Because you're younger."

David nodded.

"I wonder," said Mrs. Long, "if there's something outside of school David could do just for himself. Something his brother and sister have never even tried."

The grown-ups looked at each other.

"I don't know what that could be," Mrs. Sims said.

A wonderful feeling swelled up inside of David. He knew the answer this time! "Ballet One!" he cried.

Everyone turned to look at him.

"I'd like to go to Ballet One," he said.

"On Saturday afternoons. You could watch me on Visiting Day. So could Franny and Grandpa Sims. And J.T., when he's home."

Mrs. Long smiled at David. "I think that's a fine idea," she said. Then she looked at Mr. and Mrs. Sims. "David needs his own place to shine. Maybe then, math won't worry him so much anymore."

"Then Ballet One it is!" said Mr. Sims.

"What about Ralph and the rest of the class?" Mr. Crane asked David. "They may tease you about this, too, you know. A boy in Ballet One . . ."

"Paul and Stanley are in Ballet One," David said. "They're boys. And Ralph's wrong about lots of stuff. Besides, one bad thing shouldn't ruin all the good things. I already learned that at Ballet One."

Suddenly Mr. Crane looked *Nutcracker* happy again. "Third-graders have a lot to learn about ballet, David," he said. "And you and I are just the team to teach them!"

Chapter Ten
Thanksgiving

"I'm home!" J.T. shouted.

"J.T.!" David flew across the kitchen and wrapped his brother in a hug.

There were more hugs and kisses from Mr. and Mrs. Sims and Franny. Then J.T. headed upstairs to unpack. David was right behind him. He sat on J.T.'s bed and watched his brother unpack sweaters and shirts.

"You've grown a lot since I left," J.T. said.

David nodded. "Guess so."

J.T. seemed bigger, too. And older. In

fact, he seemed all grown-up. Suddenly David felt shy. His brother was almost a stranger. He wondered if J.T. remembered the good times they'd had together.

The door opened and Franny came in. Thanksgiving dinner smells followed her: turkey and pumpkin pie.

"J.T.," she announced, "you and I need to talk to our brother."

"We do?" J.T. asked.

"You do?" David echoed. What was Franny up to?

"We do," Franny said. She pulled out J.T.'s desk chair and sat down. "David thinks you're a math whiz and I'm a science whiz and he's not any kind of whiz at all," she told J.T. "Mama says he's been messing up his schoolwork, all because he's worrying about us."

J.T. stopped unpacking. He sat down on the bed.

For a long time, no one said anything. David picked at the bedspread. He wished he had kept his mouth shut about Franny and J.T.

The one thing in the world he didn't want was to upset his brother and sister. He thought they were terrific, and he wished they could think he was, too.

But now they thought he was dumber than ever.

Or did they?

Suddenly J.T. reached across the bed and lifted David's chin with one long finger. "Listen here, little brother," he said. "I don't want to be stuck in your head, making you think you're not good enough. I want to be in your *heart,* telling you you're one great kid."

"That goes for me, too," Franny added.

J.T. gave David's chin a little shake. "Got it?" he asked.

David grinned at them both. "Got it," he said.

Franny jumped up and replaced J.T.'s chair at his desk. "That's settled!" she said. "Now let's get J.T. unpacked before our company arrives."

"We invited Ellie and her parents," David told J.T. "And Ralph and his grandma. They don't have family in town."

"That's fine," J.T. said. "We have family to spare."

He tossed Franny shirts to hang in the closet. Then he piled David high with socks to tuck in a drawer.

"I thought you and Ralph had a fight," Franny said.

"We have lots of fights," David told her. "But we always make up."

Franny shook her head. "I don't know how you stay friends with that boy," she said. "I wouldn't have the patience for it."

David shrugged. "Ellie sometimes says I'm the only friend Ralph has."

"It must be a hard job," said J.T. "It must take a friendship *whiz* to do it!"

He tossed David a wink and the last pair of socks. David laughed as he caught them both.

"Children?" Mrs. Sims called up from the living room. "Grandpa Sims is here!"

"Last one down's a rotten egg!" J.T. yelled.

He and David and Franny dropped everything. They raced for the stairs, whooping and laughing. It was just like old times!

Grandpa Sims was waiting for them at the bottom.

"A fine-looking bunch of children," he said. "Smart, too!" His arms opened wide to gather all three of them in at once.